Jen and the Golden Pen

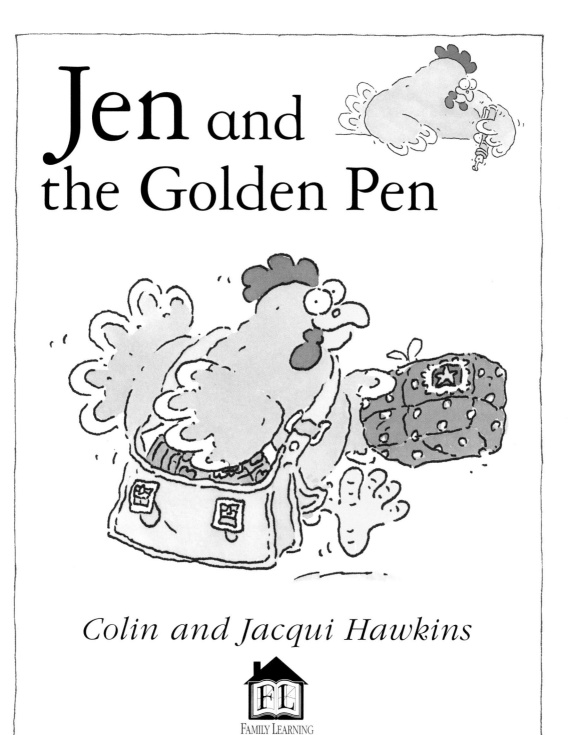

Colin and Jacqui Hawkins

FAMILY LEARNING

FAMILY LEARNING

from Dorling Kindersley

*The Family Learning mission is to support the concept
of the home as a center of learning and to help families
develop independent learning skills to last a lifetime.*

Editors: Bridget Gibbs, Fiona Munro, Constance Robinson
Designers: Chris Fraser, Lisa Hollis

Published by Family Learning

Southland Executive Park, 7800 Southland Boulevard
Orlando, Florida 32809

Dorling Kindersley registered offices:
9 Henrietta Street, Covent Garden, London WC2E 8PS

VISIT US ON THE WORLD WIDE WEB AT:
www.dk.com

ISBN 0-7894-4675-8

Color reproduction by DOT Gradations
Printed in Hong Kong by Wing King Tong

Have you heard about Jen,
who lives in the glen?
She's the hen with the pen.

Jen the hen is very bright.
Every day she loves to write.
A note here and a jot there,
Jen writes letters everywhere!
"I like nothing better than to
write a letter," says Jen,
the clever hen.

Her favorite pen is blue,
but it's not very new.
"It's scratchy and messy,
no ifs, ands, or buts —
it just drives me nuts!"
says Jen, the hen with the leaky old pen.

Jen works down in the glen
as a busy mailhen.
"My job is the best –
it beats all the rest!" says Jen.
"And without
fail, I love
sorting the
mail!"

"Here's a package for Pat, the cat with the hat, and a postcard for Tog, the sporty dog," says Jen the mailhen. "A letter for Zug the bug and a package for Zug's little blue tug," says Ken. "And here's something big for Mig, the superstar pig," says Ben.

At delivering mail, Jen's the best – through all kinds of weather, without a rest. Whether it rains or snows or the north wind blows, out she goes.

Every day, when the mail is due, Jen the mailhen always gets through.

One morning at nine, it is sunny and fine. Jen the hen, with Ken and Ben, go on their way to deliver mail for that day.

"See you later," says Jen the mailhen to the little mailmen.

"I'm going this way," says Ken.
"I'm going that way," says Ben.
Jen sets off down the road with her
heavy load. "Here's the package for Pat.
First I'll deliver that," says Jen.

"Here's a package for you,"
Jen says to Pat.
"For me? What can it be?"
says Pat, the cat with the hat.
"Open it and see," says Jen.
It's a bow tie for Pat
to wear with his hat!
"Who sent that?"
says Pat the cat.

Down the hill Jen went, with a package – and a letter that had a sweet scent. "This letter is a pretty pink. Who can it be from?" says Jen with a wink.

It's a letter for Zug
from sweet Ladybug.
This is what Ladybug
wrote to Zug:

Jen also has a surprise
for Zug's little blue tug.
"Look, Tug," says Zug.
"It's brand-new
and it's just for you!"

Dear

Don't forget our
date at 8!

Love and a hug
from your

Chug!
Chug!

TOOT!
TOOT!

Bye bye,
must fly!

Tug will
look cute!

Give us
a hoot!

As Jen goes on her way,
it becomes a foggy day.

Out of the fog
pops Tog the dog.
"Hello, Tog," says Jen.
"This postcard's for you.
Guess who it's from?
I'll give you a clue.
You got him to jog."

"I know!" says Tog.
"It's from my friend Hog!"
"What does Hog's postcard say?
Does he like being away?"
Tog reads the note, and this is
what his friend Hog wrote:

Now Jen has just one more call,
to Mig, the pig who has it all.

"A special delivery," says Jen.
"Use my pen, just sign here."
"OK, Jen," says Mig, "Oh no!"
Jen's old pen squirts blue ink
on Mig's dress of bright pink!

"I'm so sorry, what a mess.
You've got a blot on your dress!"
"It's all right, Jen, no doubt
the stain will wash out."
Then Mig wants to comfort Jen,
and offers candy to the hen.

"What a busy day!" says Jen when she gets home to her den. She makes a cup of tea and then sits down to watch TV.
KNOCK! KNOCK!
"A knock at the door, who's that for?" says Jen the tired mailhen.

It's Ken and Ben the mailmen with a package for Jen.

"A package for me!
What can it be?"
"It's special mail for the hen in the glen," say Ken and Ben to Jen.

Jen unties the knot to see the present that she got. It is a shiny golden pen for the very best mailhen.

"Wow! Can this really be for me?" says Jen the hen to the little mailmen.

"It's a little thank-you for getting the mail through," say Ken and Ben.

Then, feeling so proud, Jen read it out loud:

Lucky hen ...

... with a brand-new pen!

Dear

This pen will not blot.
We hope you like it a lot.
Love,

and

XXX

Later, Jen used her golden pen to write a thank-you note. This is what she wrote: